Read-Along
STORYBOOK AND CD

This is the story of the Little Mermaid. You can
read along with me in your book. You will know
it is time to turn the page when you hear the
chimes ring like this. . . .
Let's begin now.

Copyright © 2010 Disney Enterprises, Inc. All rights reserved.
Published by Disney Press, an imprint of Disney Book Group.
For more information address Disney Press, 114 Fifth Avenue,
New York, New York 10011-5690.

Printed in the United States of America
5 7 9 10 8 6 4

V381-8386-5-12167

Library of Congress Catalog Card Number on file.
ISBN 978-1-4231-3336-0

Visit www.disneybooks.com

Certified Chain of Custody
35% Certified Forest Content,
65% Certified Sourcing
www.sfiprogram.org
SFI-00993
SUSTAINABLE
FORESTRY
INITIATIVE

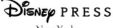
New York

Once upon a time, a little mermaid named Ariel frolicked below the ocean. She loved to explore sunken ships and look for lost objects. She called to her friend Flounder, a yellow fish. "Come on, Flounder! I'm sure this old boat has lots of human treasure aboard."

"I'm not g-g-going in there! It's spooky!"

"Don't be such a guppy! Follow me!"

When Ariel swam inside the ship's cabin, she discovered a fork. "Oh, my gosh! Have you ever seen anything so wonderful?"

Ariel swam to the water's surface and found her seagull friend. "Scuttle, do you know what this is?" She handed him the fork.

"Judging from my expert knowledge of humans, it's obviously a . . . a . . . *dinglehopper*! Humans use these to straighten their hair."

"Thanks, Scuttle! It's perfect for my collection." And with that, Ariel dove excitedly back underwater.

Soon, Ariel arrived in an undersea grotto where she kept her treasures from the human world. She hid her collection there because her father, King Triton, forbade merpeople from having any contact with humans.

That night, Ariel saw strange lights shimmering over the ocean. She and Flounder swam up to investigate.

At the surface, they found Scuttle flying over a large sailing ship. "Some celebration, huh, sweetie? It's the birthday of the human they call Prince Eric."

Forgetting her father's rule, Ariel peered in amazement at the young man on the deck. "I've never seen a human this close. He's very handsome."

She watched as Eric's adviser, Grimsby, presented the prince with a birthday gift.

Meanwhile, far beneath the ocean, the wicked sea witch, Ursula, used her magic to spy on Ariel. Ursula was bitter because King Triton had banished her from his kingdom for her evildoing.

"My, my . . . the daughter of the great sea king, Triton, in love with a human! This headstrong, lovesick girl may be the key to my revenge on Triton."

On the surface, a sudden storm whipped across the ocean. The prince took charge. "Stand fast! Secure the rigging!"

Without warning, a huge bolt of lightning struck the vessel. Ariel watched in horror. "Eric's been knocked into the water! I've got to save him!"

With the raging storm swirling around her, Ariel desperately searched for Eric. "Where is he? If I don't find him soon. . . . Wait, there he is!"

She took hold of Eric and, using all her strength, managed to pull him to the surface.

As the storm calmed down, Ariel dragged the unconscious prince to shore. "He's still breathing. He must be alive."

Just then, a crab named Sebastian scuttled across the sand. He was the sea king's music director and adviser. "Ariel, get away from that human! Your father forbids contact with them, remember?"

"But Sebastian, why can't I be part of his world?" And she sang about longing to be with Prince Eric forever.

Back in the king's palace, Triton noticed Ariel floating about as if in a dream. Suspicious of his daughter's behavior, Triton summoned Sebastian. The crab told him the truth about the shipwreck and the prince.

"Ariel is in love with a *human?*"

King Triton went straight to Ariel's grotto. "How many times have I told you to stay away from those fish-eating barbarians. Humans are dangerous!"

"But, Daddy, I love Eric!"

King Triton would not listen.

Raising his trident, the sea king destroyed all of Ariel's human treasures. Then he stormed off, leaving the little mermaid in tears.

As she wept, two eels slithered up to Ariel and startled her. "Don't be scared. . . . We represent someone who can help you!"

They told her they had been sent by Ursula, who could use her powers to solve Ariel's troubles.

Ariel was so upset that she followed the eels to Ursula's den. The sea witch offered Ariel a deal. "I'll grant you three days as a human to win your prince. Before sunset on the third day, you must get him to kiss you. If you do, he's yours forever. But if you don't—you'll be mine!"

Ariel took a deep breath and nodded. The sea witch smiled deviously. "Oh, yes, I almost forgot. We haven't discussed payment. I'm not asking much. All I want is—your voice!"

Ariel agreed, and Ursula completed the spell. The evil witch captured Ariel's voice in a seashell locket and turned the mermaid into a human.

With the help of Sebastian and Flounder, Ariel used her new legs to swim awkwardly to shore. She wrapped herself in an old sail. Then she saw Prince Eric walking toward her with his dog, Max. "Down, Max, down! I'm awfully sorry, miss."

Ariel opened her mouth to answer, forgetting that her voice was gone. Eric helped her to her feet.

"Well, the least I can do is make amends for my dog's bad manners. Come on. I'll take you to the palace and get you cleaned up."

The following afternoon, Eric took Ariel for a rowboat ride across a lagoon. Sebastian knew that Ariel only had one more day to get the prince to kiss her, or she would become Ursula's prisoner forever. So he began conducting a sea-creature chorus to set the mood. "C'mon and kiss the girl. . . . The music's working!"

As the prince bent toward her, the boat suddenly tipped, and both Ariel and Eric fell into the water!

From her ocean lair, Ursula saw them tumble into the lagoon.
"That was too close for comfort! I can't let Ariel get away that easily!"
She began concocting a magic potion that would transform her
into a human. "Soon Triton's daughter will be mine!"

The next morning, Scuttle flew into Ariel's room. The prince had announced his wedding! Ariel's heart skipped a beat at the thought that she had won Eric's love. But when she hurried downstairs, she saw him introducing Grimsby to a mysterious, dark-haired maiden.

"Vanessa saved my life. We're going to be married on board ship at sunset."

Ariel was heartbroken. Who was this girl that Eric had suddenly fallen in love with?

A little while later, Ariel and her friends were watching the wedding ship leave the harbor.

Suddenly, Scuttle crash-landed beside them. "When I flew over the boat, I saw Vanessa's reflection in a mirror. She's the sea witch in disguise!"

Flounder helped Ariel swim out to the ship as fast as possible. They arrived just before sunset! Before Vanessa could say *I do*, Scuttle and an army of his friends attacked her.

In the scuffle, the maiden's seashell necklace crashed to the deck, freeing Ariel's voice.

Ariel smiled at the prince. "Oh, Eric, I wanted to tell you—"

Ursula grinned. "You're too late! The sun has set!"

As Ariel felt her body changing back into a mermaid, Ursula pulled her into the water. King Triton confronted the sea witch and made a deal with her to take his daughter's place as Ursula's slave. Instantly, he lost his powers and turned into a helpless sea creature. Ursula became queen of the ocean!

Just then, Prince Eric threw a harpoon at the sea witch to try to stop her. But it simply grazed her arm. Ursula snatched up the king's powerful trident. "You little fool!"

All of a sudden, Ursula turned into an enormous monster and stirred the waters into a deadly whirlpool.

Several old sunken ships rose to the surface. The prince struggled aboard one of them and plunged the sharp prow through the sea witch, destroying her. The mighty force sent Eric flying into the ocean, but he managed to swim to shore before collapsing in exhaustion. King Triton was transformed back into a merman and regained his powers.

Moments later, as the unconscious prince lay on the beach, Ariel
perched on a rock and gazed at him. King Triton and Sebastian
watched from afar. "She really does love him, doesn't she, Sebastian?"
The sea king wanted his daughter to be happy. So he waved his
trident, and Ariel was once again human.

The next day, she and Prince Eric were married aboard a wedding ship. As they kissed, the humans and merpeople sent up a joyful cheer. Ariel and Eric sailed off into the sunset, knowing that they would live happily ever after.